SUHO and the WHITE HORSE

A Legend of Mongolia

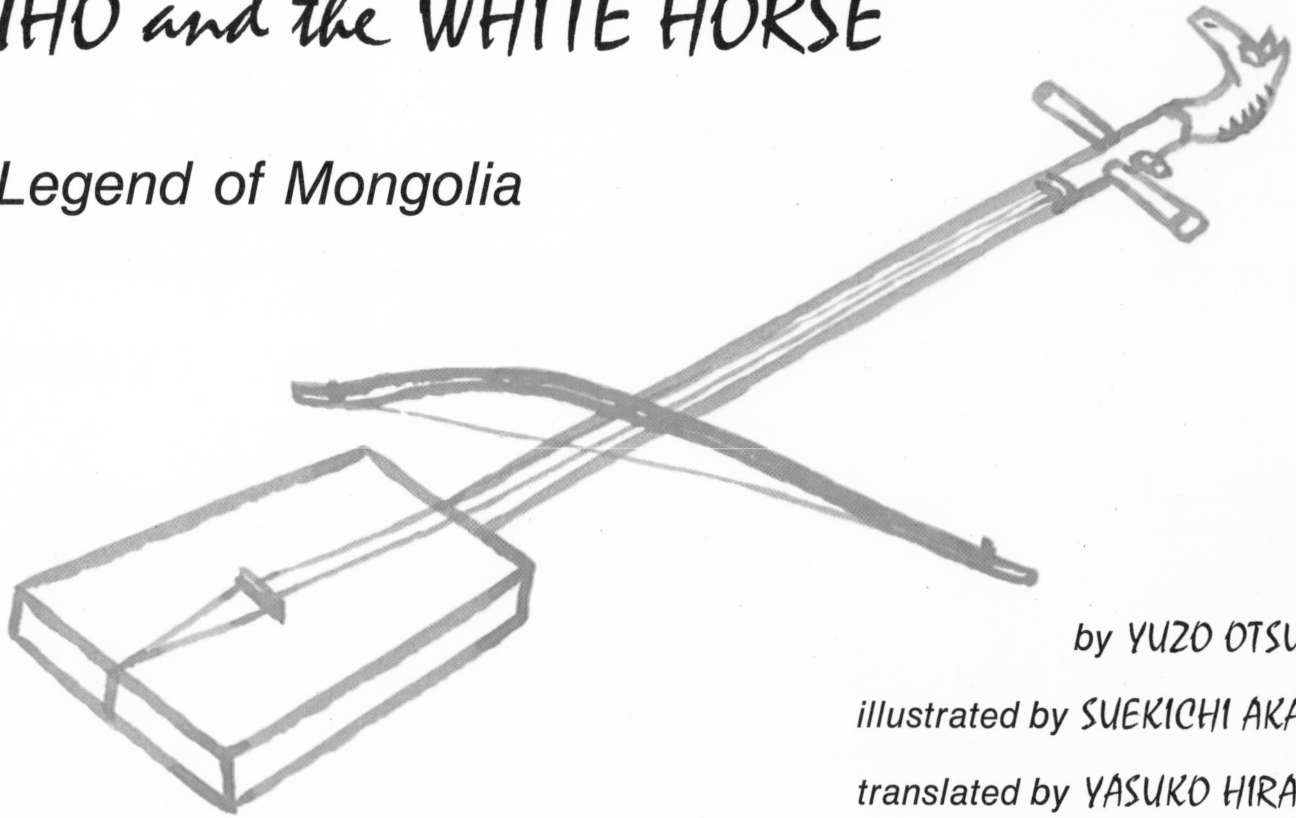

by YUZO OTSUKA
illustrated by SUEKICHI AKABA
translated by YASUKO HIRAWA

THE BOBBS-MERRILL COMPANY, INC. Indianapolis New York

In the heart of Asia, north of China, lies the ancient land of Mongolia. For ages past, its broad steppes and grasslands have been the home of brave horsemen and hardy shepherd folk. Many of them are skilled at playing a beautiful instrument called the horse-head fiddle. The instrument takes its name from the small figure of a horse's head, carved at the top of its neck.

If the horse-head fiddle could speak, this is the tale it would tell.

Long ago, in a tent in the middle of the steppes, lived Suho, a poor shepherd lad, and his grandmother. Though scarcely more than a boy, Suho worked as hard as any man, going out into the grassy plains each day to watch over his small flock of sheep.

One evening, Suho failed to return at the usual time. The sun sank behind the distant mountains, darkness fell, and still there was no sign of Suho. His grandmother and her friends were worried. Suddenly they saw him, carrying a newborn foal in his arms.

Beaming with happiness, he told them he had found the foal in the plains. He had searched everywhere for the foal's master, or for his mother, but had found no one. Rather than leave the foal lying there, where the wolves would be certain to get him, the boy brought the little foal home.

Suho devoted himself to caring for the colt. Days went by, one after the other, and the colt grew into a splendid, spirited yearling, with a gleaming white coat. Everyone who saw him admired his beauty. Suho was proud of his horse, and loved him dearly.

Late one night, awakened suddenly by strange cries, Suho ran out to the sheepfold. A large wolf was straining to get at the sheep. But the white horse, rearing and bucking savagely, kept him away from them.

Suho took up a stick and drove the wolf away. Then he hastened to the side of his horse, who was wet and shivering, to dry him and comfort him. Caressing his white horse, speaking tenderly, he said, "White horse, you have fought well and bravely tonight. I am proud of you."

Many months had passed when one spring day exciting news came to the village. The governor had called for a great race to be held in the city. The rider of the fastest horse was to win the hand of the governor's daughter in marriage.

When the herdsmen heard this, they urged Suho to enter the race.

On the day of the race, Suho mounted his beloved white horse, turned his face toward the governor's city, and rode off across the grasslands.

People had come from far and near to see the race. At the field, seated in a large pavilion, surrounded by servants, was the governor himself.

At the sign to start, the horsemen swung their riding crops and galloped away.

Off they ran, swift as birds in flight, with Suho's horse in the lead.

"The white horse has won!" cried the governor. "Summon its rider to me."

When the governor saw Suho standing before him, he was greatly disappointed. Never would he give the hand of his daughter in marriage to a low-born shepherd lad.

"Here are three pieces of silver," he said. "Go now, and leave the white horse with me."

Suho stared at the governor.

"I have come here to run in a race," he said, "not to sell my horse."

"How dare you speak to me that way!" said the governor. "Guards!" he cried. "Beat the wretch, and send him on his way."

With raised clubs, guards attacked Suho from every direction, then left him lying on the ground.

A friend who had come to watch the race carried Suho home.

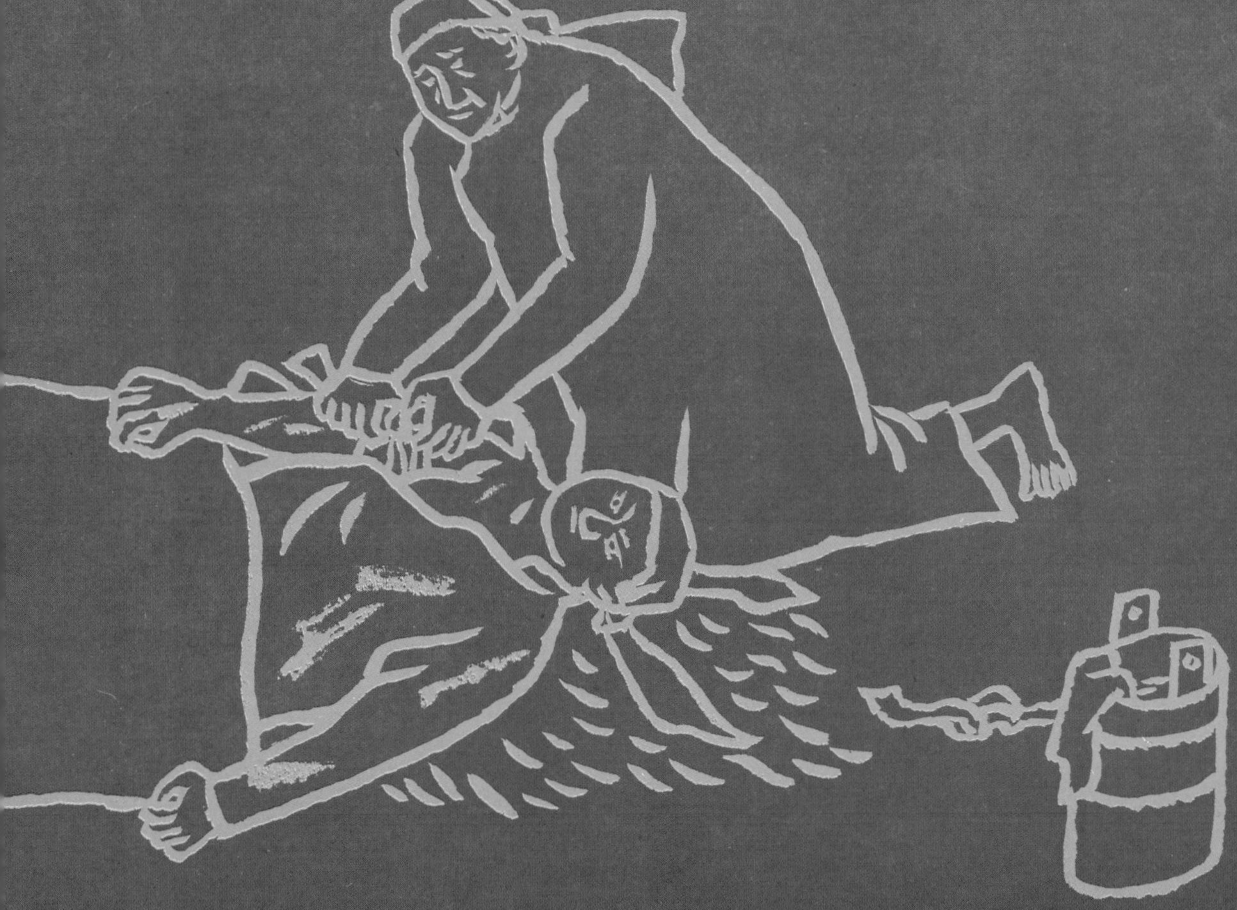

Lovingly and with skill Suho's grandmother tended his wounds, never leaving his side. In time, his wounds began to heal. But nothing could heal the sorrow in his heart. His white horse was gone. Where was he? How was he? Suho could think of nothing else.

As for the governor, he was so proud of his new possession that one day he invited all the nobles to a grand banquet, to show off his new white horse.

At the height of the feast, the white horse, now richly saddled and bridled, was brought in. The governor approached the horse, ready to mount him.

No sooner had he heaved himself into the saddle than the horse reared up and sent him tumbling to the ground. Before anyone could stop him, the white horse galloped away.

"Shoot!" cried the governor, struggling to his feet. "Don't let him get away!"

Their bows drawn, the guards sent a stream of arrows into the air. One after the other, the arrows struck home. Although his back and sides were pierced with arrows, the white horse raced on.

Late that evening, Suho heard a noise outside.

"What can that be?" he asked.

His grandmother went to the door.

"The horse!" she cried. "It is our white horse!"

Rushing outside, Suho saw his horse, covered with arrows. The horse limped up to him, brushed his nose against Suho's face, then fell to the ground.

Suho wept as he removed one arrow after the other from his horse's flanks. "Don't ever leave me again," he sobbed. But the white horse grew weaker and weaker. His breathing grew faint; the luster faded from his eyes. When Suho had removed the last arrow, the white horse closed his eyes for the last time.

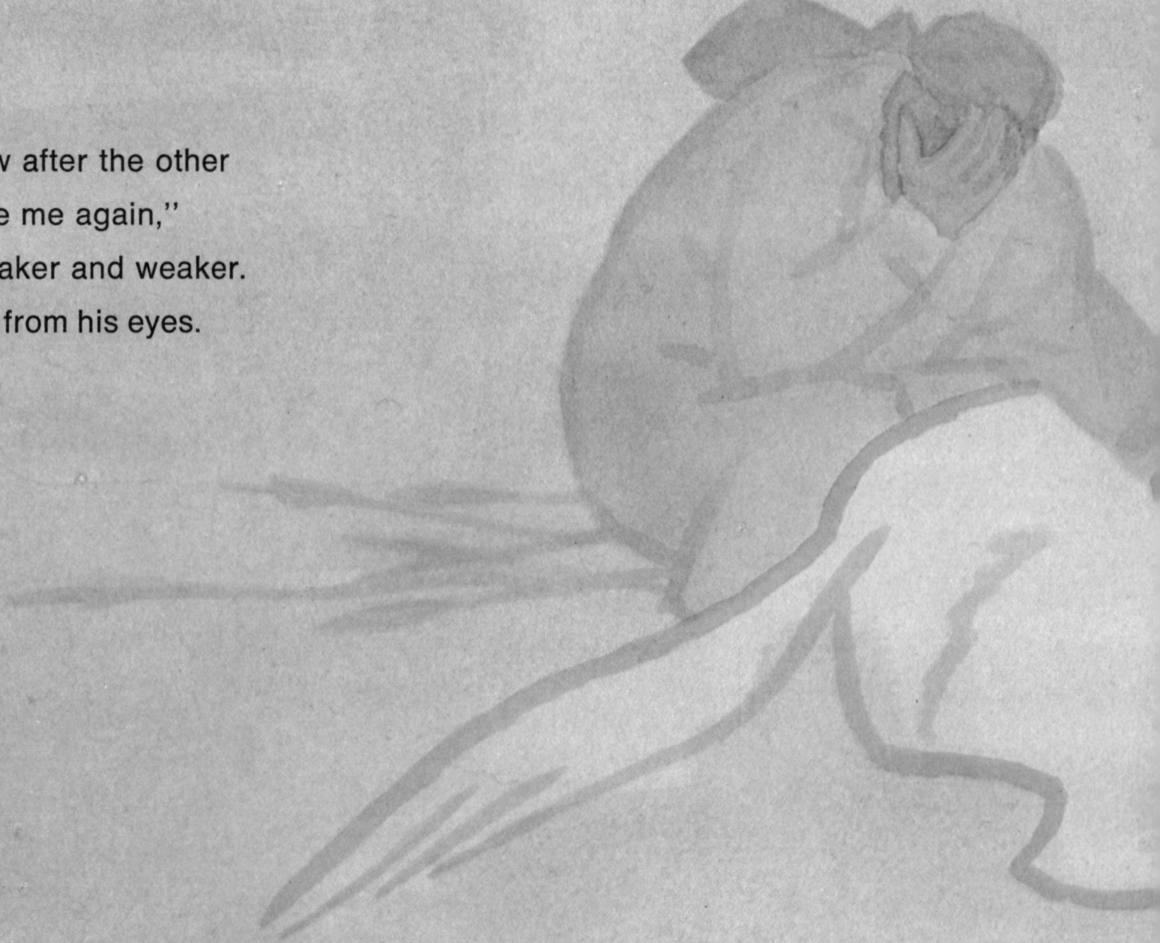

That night, Suho could not go to sleep. He wept all night long. Toward morning, exhausted, he dozed off. His beloved white horse appeared to him in a dream. "Suho, do not mourn for me," he said. "Take my bones, my hide, and my sinews, and with them make a musical instrument. This will allow me to be at your side forever, and bring you happiness and peace."

In the morning, when he awoke, Suho recalled the words in his dream and set about at once to fashion an instrument from the bones, sinews, hide and hair of his beloved white horse.

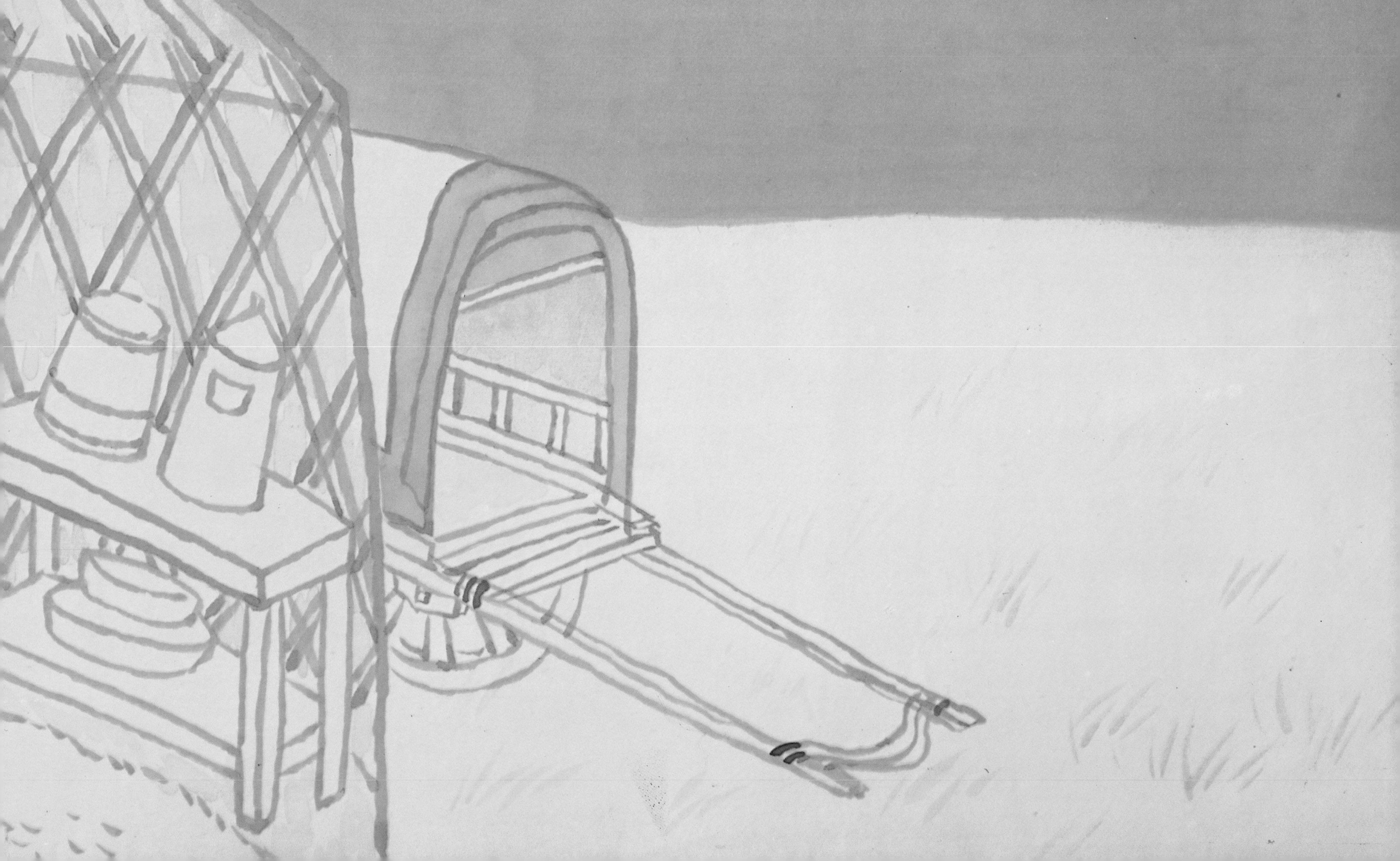

When he was finished, he had made a beautiful instrument. It was a kind of fiddle, ornamented by the carved figure of a horse's head. Wherever Suho went, he took the horse-head fiddle with him. The sweet music it made when he drew the bow across its strings filled his heart with joy. Sometimes he could almost see the white horse standing there, looking at him.
At such times, the tones of the fiddle were mellower and more beautiful than ever.

Before long, others in the village began to make horse-head fiddles like the one Suho had created. In time, their music could be heard everywhere in the grasslands of Mongolia, bringing peace and contentment to the hearts of the shepherd folk who gathered in the evenings to listen to their sweet song.

The BOBBS-MERRILL Company, Inc.
A Subsidiary of Howard W. Sams & Co., Inc.
Publishers Indianapolis Kansas City New York

First English language edition published in the United States of America
by The Bobbs-Merrill Company, Inc.
Printed and manufactured in Japan
Library of Congress catalog card number: 79-75139